Parents and Caregivers,

Stone Arch Readers are designed to ⬚⬚⬚⬚⬚⬚⬚⬚⬚⬚⬚
experiences, as well as opportunities to develop vocabulary,
literacy skills, and comprehension. Here are a few ways to
support your beginning reader:

• Talk with your child about the ideas addressed in the story.

• Discuss each illustration, mentioning the characters, where they
  are, and what they are doing.

• Read with expression, pointing to each word. You may want to
  read the whole story through and then revisit parts of the story to
  ensure that the meanings of words or phrases are understood.

• Talk about why the character did what he or she did and what
  your child would do in that situation.

• Help your child connect with characters and events in the story.

Remember, reading with your child should be fun, not forced. Each
moment spent reading with your child is a priceless investment in
his or her literacy life.

Gail Saunders-Smith, Ph.D.

Stone Arch Readers

are published by Stone Arch Books
a Capstone Imprint
1710 Roe Crest Drive
North Mankato, Minnesota 56003
www.capstonepub.com

Library of Congress Cataloging-in-Publication Data
Crow, Melinda Melton.
Rocky and Daisy and the birthday party / by Melinda Melton Crow; illustrated by Eva Sassin.
p. cm. — (Stone Arch readers: My two dogs)
Summary: It is their human friend Owen's birthday, and Rocky and Daisy want to participate in
the preparations—and share in the food.
ISBN 978-1-4342-6011-6 (library binding) — ISBN 978-1-4342-6205-9 (pbk.)
1. Dogs—Juvenile fiction. 2. Birthday parties—Juvenile fiction. [1. Dogs—Fiction. 2. Birthday
parties—Fiction. 3. Parties—Fiction.] I. Sassin, Eva, ill. II. Title.
PZ7.C88536Rov 2013
813.6—dc23   2012047366

Reading Consultants:
Gail Saunders-Smith, Ph.D.
Melinda Melton Crow, M.Ed.
Laurie K. Holland, Media Specialist

Designer: Kristi Carlson

Printed in China by Nordica.
0413/CA21300422
032013
007226NORDF13

Rocky and Daisy
and the
Birthday Party

by **Melinda Melton Crow**

illustrated by **Eva Sassin**

STONE ARCH BOOKS
a capstone imprint

MY TWO DOGS

I'm Owen, and these are Rocky and Daisy, my two dogs.

ROCKY LIKES:

- Chasing squirrels
- Playing with other dogs
- Chewing things
- Running with me when I ride my bike

DAISY LIKES:

- Playing ball
- Listening to stories
- Resting on the furniture
- Eating yummy treats

Rocky and Daisy loved their
friend Owen. He fed them.

He brushed them.

And of course, he played with them.

Owen treated his dogs special.
Now it was Owen's turn to be
treated special. It was Owen's
birthday!

"Happy birthday, Owen!"
said Rocky and Daisy. Owen
grinned.

Owen was excited for his
birthday party. His friends were
coming over for a pool party.

They would roast hot dogs
over a bonfire.

They would eat cake.

Rocky and Daisy were excited for the party, too.

"Yum," Daisy said. "I like hot dogs."

"Me too," said Rocky. "And I like swimming with Owen's friends."

It was time to get ready for the party. Dad and Owen filled the balloons with water. They put them into buckets.

"Look, Rocky," said Daisy. She picked up a balloon. It broke and splashed water all over.

"Oh, Daisy!" said Dad. "Those are for the party."

Mom threw sticks into a pile for the fire pit. Rocky loved to chase sticks. He brought them back to Mom.

"No, Rocky!" said Mom.
"Those are for the bonfire."

"Come here, Rocky and Daisy," said Owen. "Stay inside until the party begins."

Rocky and Daisy did not like being inside. They looked out the door and cried.

"No fair," said Daisy.

Owen's friends came. They
jumped into the pool. Rocky
and Daisy howled and barked.
They wanted to swim with
the boys.

Finally, Dad let them out.
Rocky ran and jumped into the
pool. Daisy used the steps.

"Time for the water balloon toss," shouted Dad.

"Yea!" yelled Rocky. He ran back and forth trying to catch one.

Daisy did not want to play with the balloons. She just watched.

Soon everyone was hungry.
The boys roasted hot dogs over
the fire. They were so good!

Daisy begged for a hot dog.
"Sorry," said Mom. "You have
to eat dog food."

Then Mom brought out
Owen's birthday cake. It was
covered with candles.

"Look, Rocky," said Daisy. "We are on the cake!"

Everyone sang "Happy Birthday" to Owen. Then he blew out the candles.

Mom gave Rocky and Daisy a special cake, too. "This is a cake just for dogs," she said.

"Yum," said Daisy. The cake
tasted like peanut butter.

"It is good," said Rocky. He
licked the plate clean.

After the party, Owen floated
on a raft with Rocky and Daisy.

"That was the best birthday party ever!" said Owen. Rocky and Daisy agreed.

THE END

STORY WORDS

special	roast	buckets
excited	bonfire	howled

Total Word Count: 406

READ MORE

ROCKY AND DAISY ADVENTURES!